This Little Hippo
book belongs to

For Auntie Lily, Auntie Annie, Uncle Bill, Auntie Amy,
Cousin Malcolm, Auntie Ethel, Ronald and Sylvia,
all the other Waterhouses and Harry Venning.
~ L.W.

To all my Aunties and Uncles.
~ A.R.

Scholastic Children's Books,
Commonwealth House, 1-19 New Oxford Street,
London WC1A 1NU, UK
a division of Scholastic Ltd

London • New York • Toronto • Sydney • Auckland
Mexico City • New Delhi • Hong Kong

First published in the UK in 2000 by Little Hippo,
an imprint of Scholastic Ltd

Text copyright © Lynda Waterhouse, 2000
Illustrations copyright © Arthur Robins, 2000

ISBN 0 439 01393 3

Printed in Italy

JUST LIKE

by **Lynda Waterhouse**

illustrated by **Arthur Robins**

Little Hippo

When I was just a few days old, all the Aunties and Uncles and Grandad came round to the house.

They stood around eating sandwiches.

"Sam looks just like you," Great Aunt
Bertha said to Dad.

They all munched and nodded . . .

. . . except Grandad.
He was playing outside.

On Christmas Day, all the Aunties and Uncles brought presents to the house.

They sat round eating mince pies.
"He's got eyes just like his mother's,"
Auntie Rita said to Mum.

They all nodded . . .

. . . except Grandad.
He was racing down the hill.

At Cousin Julie's wedding,
I wouldn't kiss
Auntie Joan.

Great Uncle Bernard cried,
"He's shy, just like
Uncle Norris."
"Ah, look at him,"
they all sighed . . .

. . . except Grandad.

He was practising his magic tricks.

At Cousin Nigel's birthday
party, I danced on my own
in the middle of the hall.

"What a show off!" chuckled Uncle
Norris. "Just like Great Uncle Bernard."
Everyone burst out laughing
and clapped . . .

. . . except Grandad.
He was standing on his chair.

At the school concert, I played my recorder in the band.

I won a prize and when I collected my certificate, Auntie Joan said, "Musical. Just like Auntie Rita. She's musical."
Everyone cheered loudly . . .

. . . except Grandad.
He was busy.

At the seaside my legs
turned bright red!

"Delicate skin," tutted Auntie Vera.
"Just like Great Aunt Bertha."
"Dear, oh dear," they all said . . .

. . . except Grandad.
He was winning prizes.

On my birthday, all my Aunties
and Uncles gathered round.
Dad said, "Make a wish, Sam."
Everyone smiled . . .

. . . except me!

"I wish that you would all stop
saying that every single thing
I do is just like somebody else!
I am me. And the only person
I am just like is ME!"

I shouted so loudly that
the candles blew out . . .

The jellies wobbled.

The sausages shivered.

The crisps curled.

Nobody said a word.

Until Auntie Vera shook her head, tutted and said, "Making a big show of himself just like . . ."

"ME!" yelled Grandad.
And then he winked.

"Come on, Sam," smiled Grandad,
"it's your birthday . . ."

"LET'S HAVE SOME FUN!"